Lily & Lucille

Dedicated to my Mother

Valerie Marchant

Prologue

Although the story of Lily and Lucille is one of fiction, the characters and places are real. My inspiration for the story comes from my Mother Valerie Marchant, who lived on the island of Jersey, along with her parents Raymond and Dorothy, and her sister Janette.

Raymond Crees was a gardener for the Earl of Jersey, he was a very tenacious and a handsome character, who soon attracted the attention of the conservative and shy Dorothy Bisson, they eventually married, and had two beautiful Daughters, where they lived a happy and harmonious life for many years, regrettably, their idyllic life on the island of Jersey came to an end, when they made the brave decision to leave, in search of new beginnings in England.

Raymond Crees only wished the best for his family, and had arrived at the conclusion that a life in Great Britain, held better opportunities for them all. Even to this day, my Mother recalls with irremediable sorrow, how she felt as they boarded the ferry bound for Great Britain.

My Mother stood on the deck, in what had seemed the darkest of nights, watching on with a great wrench of sadness, as Jersey disappeared into the horizon.

Fortunately for my Mum, after adapting to her new life in Great Britain, it transpired it was the right thing to do, and she soon realized that a future in Great Britain held brighter opportunities, than the life she had left behind on the island of Jersey, that said, it remains forever in her heart.

The Past

As a child I was truly captivated by the stories of the island, and the people on it, an island steeped in history, with its forts and castles, as well as the traces of dark times, resilience, liberation, and celebration. My Grandparents very rarely spoke of the Island's occupation, but when they did, it depicted stories of resistance, rebellion and defiance, but also of hunger, survival, and deprivation.

The Channel Islands was the only part of the British Isles to be occupied by German forces in world war two, a German pilot landed at Guernsey airport in 1940.

The pilot then returned to France and notified his superiors that the Island appeared to be undefended. The very next day, planes arrived bringing German troops to the Islands, and the occupation began, and everyone who had stayed, became trapped for five years.

That was until the 9th of May in 1945, when news of freedom broke, giddy ranks of people flocked into Saint Helier, where the Union Jack was raised above the Pomme D'or hotel.

The hotel still remains to this day, gazing proudly across to what is now called "Liberation Square," a bronze sculpture was erected for the 50th anniversary, and depicts seven islanders lifting a Union Jack to the heavens.

The experience and memory of the occupation lies deep within the island of Jersey, with many of the islanders, impacted and displaced by the conflict, the ghosts of the occupation still remain in every corner of the island.

Like many of the islanders, my Grandparents cherished liberty and freedom, and as time went by, Jersey was restored to its former glory.

Raymond & Dorothy Crees

The Present

On many occasions as a child, our family would travel back to the island, sailing through the night on my dad's boat, I would stay awake whilst my siblings slept soundly. As dawn broke, my mother would be seated at the bow of the boat, her face a picture of sheer joy, as the island welcomed her back into its very heart.

I have always been intrigued by the unique and captivating island of Jersey, and I do believe the island itself was my true inspiration for wanting to become a writer. I loved this treasure trove of an island, my imagination would run high, with the array of spellbinding castles of kings in exile, swashbuckling pirates, and the "Forgotten forest" full of unusual trees, plants, and exotic fauna

We would start our day at the majestic Mont Orgueil castle, and explore the endless shorelines of shimmering blue waters at Grouville Bay.

At low tide, the bay would be transformed into a vast lunar landscape of gullies and rock pools, where we would spend hours searching for crabs that skulked under the clumps of seaweed.

I can't say for sure what my favorite place was, each had their own infinite charm, Beuport bay was just glorious with Its crystal blue waters, flanked by cliffs of pink granite, but I also loved the epic drama of Saint Ouen's, with its expansive sweeping bay, this was a place where you could experience a true sense of space, along with nature's mighty power, as the waves pounded the coast.

But if I really had to choose, it would be Portelet bay, which is how I came to have my name, and why I feel such an infinity for this place, a bay that evokes the aura of a long-lost paradise, the treasure at the end of Jersey's beautiful coastline, minus the swashbuckling pirates.

The favorite part of my day in Jersey however, was when we would climb up the path to the cliffs that towered over the pretty harbor of St Helier, the view from the top was always the greatest finale to behold, as the day came to a close.

We would be huddled together on the cliffs, under a star filled sky of sparkling diamonds, the argent-silver orb of the moon would slowly rise up from the sea, casting shimmering moonlit lasers, turning the undulating sea below it into a melted platinum, then we would watch as the sky played its final act, engulfing the sea into its blue velvety cloak

To us those holidays were a time of joy, but for my Mum, with every night that passed, her sadness became evident as the holiday came to an end. On the last night on the cliffs, her arms remained folded protectively around her body, traces of tears in her eyes, as she gazed silently across the channel, aware as dawn broke, we would be once more, sailing away from her beloved island of Jersey.

Chapter One

In the honeyed light of the evening, Lucile worked tirelessly in her garden, stopping momentarily to gaze over at the sea. The ocean seemed endless as the whispers of the warm sea breeze skipped over the lulling waves below. Lucille breathed in the salty aroma, which carried in with it a feeling of tranquility and calm.

From a distance she could hear the thundering raspy echoes of the waves, as they churned and crashed against the rocks.
The storm panes of La Corbiere lighthouse glittered in the sun, as it rose up proudly and protectively over the dark rocks of the tidal island, a storm watcher and sentinel, that stood through the island's sunsets, and weathered the many Atlantic storms, guiding ships and helping them navigate through the vast waters. Lucille took off her straw hat, releasing her chestnut brown hair, which cascaded in loose soft waves down to her waist, the warm sea breeze eddied and swirled, rippling the light lemon fabric of her sundress. At the age of forty, Lucile had still

retained her youthful looks and small frame, she was "pixie small," with a fetchingly crescent waist, and jutting collarbones, her skin pale and silken, contrasting the whimsical pop of green in her opalescent eyes."

Lucille had never married, or had a family to talk of, choosing a solitary life with no schedule or dependent's, apart from her beloved cat Lily. Her traumatic past had led her to gain confidence in her own authenticity, and she at last, had been able to leave the traumatic past behind her.

Lucille found being alone, a true luxury in life, a life where she had striven to carve out time in the space around her, a place where she had found peace and solitude to unwind, shunning the external influences of the outside world.

Lucille's sanctuary was her garden, an oasis that was wild and unkempt, the paths awash with sea shingle, crumbling chandlery and sea holly.

It was an idyllic refuge of her own creation, where she could relax and unwind. Lucille felt safe here as she relaxed against the trunk of an old ash tree in the secluded part of her garden, breathing in the scent of the honeysuckle that festooned the hedges with its lady-like perfume.

As the sun rose, it brought with it a potpourri of scents, a sweet mix of jasmine, grass vapour, and blossoms, that floated in on the sea breeze.

Rejuvenated and relaxed after a day's gardening, Lucille would gather up her tools, and make her way to the topmost part of the garden, that backed onto her tiny cliff side cottage, to see where her cat Lily had got to.

As always, Lily was asleep in her favorite place in the garden, sleeping soundly on the wall, absorbing the sun heat from the bricks, with her head nestled against the verdant moss cushions. Lucille crouched down and stroked the soft fur between her ears. Lily was twelve   years old now, and despite the challenges of aging, she had continued to navigate the world around her with determination and grace, but it was clear to Lucile that she was no longer so agile. Maybe Lucille had just refused to see the changes along the way, but Lily had gone from jumping from the highest perch, to having difficulty in keeping her legs firmly on the ground.

Lucille had tried to pass off her sudden sliding on the kitchen floor, but Lily no longer had much traction.

Her back legs had become bow-legged, which was a definite sign of arthritis. And although she could no longer leap and bound with the same agility as her younger self, she still looked really good for her age, no doubt from the boundless supply of love and affection, along with the fresh fish caught from the bay below. Lucille bent forward and scooped Lily up into her arms, "well" she said "It looks like one of us, has been doing a great deal more than just lazing around, and is most definitely ready for dinner.

After a sumptuous meal of fresh fish, caught early that morning from the bay below, Lucille carried Lily to their favorite spot on the east side of the island. She sat down on the soft grass of a rocky promontory that looked over the pretty harbor of St Helier.

The Port below was a hive of activity, with fisherman and mariners securing their vessels, which bobbed and rolled on the waves, their masts all chinking, creating their very own nautical chimes. It was here that Lucille would reflect on her life, and the traumatic events that had led her to the island of Jersey.

The vast channel before her, remaining a barrier and protector, from the ghosts that had darkened each and every street corner back in Paris. This was a life she had once treasured, that was until that fateful day, when everything she loved was taken away from her. Lucille drew in a sharp breath of anguish, at the memories and the events of the traumatic day, that remained indelibly etched in her memory.

Lucille had once been a famous ballet dancer, who had trained in the Parisian Opera house, she had become one of the most celebrated dancers in the whole of France, until one day, when a tragic event changed not only her life as she knew it, but her career as a dancer too.

Tragically, Lucille had lost both her parents, whilst they were away on a weekend break in the Alps, they had been driving along the winding and narrow road, carved into the cliff of the mountain, they had not seen the oncoming car speeding around the corner towards them, and with the road so narrow, they simply had no place to pass.

Worried for their safety, after not returning home on the Monday morning, Lucille had rushed off first thing to her local police station, and filled out a missing person's report.

The days that followed were torturous, the ticking of the clock in the lounge seemed unbelievably loud, as she paced back and forth, every few minutes running to the window, at the sound of a car parking up.

Exhausted after days of watching and waiting, Lucille went into her parents' bedroom, and laid down on the side of the bed where her Mother would normally be sleeping. Lucille wrapped her arms protectively around her knees, and drifted off momentarily, but the trauma in her brain was worse than being awake.

The following morning she resumed the same position on the sofa, watching the clock slowly ticking away, but sadly so, they never arrived home that day, or the days that followed.

Chapter Two

Jacque and Camille couldn't remember the last time they had enjoyed a weekend away so much, driving along the scenic and winding roads through the Alps.

The "Tour du Mont Blanc," had been so breathtaking, with its magnificent views of the snow-capped peaks, and sparkling glacial lakes, nestled amongst the beautiful alpine forest.

It had been a much-needed break away from the city, enjoying the freedom and space as they went hiking through the lush alpine meadows.

They had stayed in a beautiful chalet in one of the charming mountain villages, sleeping soundly under the steep gable roof, enjoying the silence of the mountain, whilst they had slept in a bed with the softest of mattresses, snuggled into the corner under the large eaves, just enjoying each other's company

As the sun rose, they sat out on the stone balcony, sharing a breakfast of coffee and croissants, whilst taking in the stunning views in front of them.

To Camille It felt like being In a giant postcard. It was so insanely beautiful and surreal, the mountain views had taken her breath away on the first morning of waking.

They had both felt rejuvenated and refreshed after the holiday, and were both looking forward to seeing their beloved daughter Lucille. The joy was ever more heightened, as they had news that would no doubt bring a great deal of happiness to her.

Jacque placed their travel bags into the back of their little red Citroen, and checked the oil, whilst Camille washed up the dishes from breakfast, before they both climbed into the front seat of their car.

Jacque smiled across at Camille as she fiddled with the knob on the radio, and burst along in chorus to the sounds of Larry Greco, as they made their way down the graveled path of the driveway.

Jacque drove at a leisurely pace, as they engineered their way through the twists and turns of the Col de la Bonette road, fully aware that a two-thousand-meter drop lay below them.

Jacque's eyes remained firmly fixed on the road ahead as they travelled along, he did not see the black Coupe as it came roaring at a furious speed around the bend, or the driver behind the wheel, as he lost control of his car.

The collision was so sudden and immediate, that not a gasp of air left their bodies, as the front of their car crumpled with the force of the impact, thrusting two-foot of metal back into the car.

The windshield imploded, showering them both with deadly slivers of glass. Both the driving wheel and dashboard compacted into one mangled mess.

The rear side passenger door tore free from its hinges and the front two wheels were sent spinning as they ploughed through the guard-rail and over the side of the mountain.

The metal of the car groaned like the final cry of a wounded beast as it shuddered and crashed to the ground below.

There were no fond goodbyes, nor a fleeting last glance of love as the car crashed into the rocks, the impact was so severe that both Jacque and Camille had died instantaneously. For weeks the police had searched for her beloved parents, until sadly so, the car, along with her parent's bodies, were discovered at the bottom of a steep and rocky Gorge, by a group of walkers who had been out on an early morning hike.

Chapter Three

Lucille had never forgotten that fateful Friday morning, as she stood washing her breakfast dishes in the sink, watching out of the window as the sun slowly rose up over the city.

A small glimmer of hope remained, but then they came. She remembered each second unfold like it was yesterday, the police car pulling up outside, then the heavy footsteps pounding on the stairs, her heart beating faster and faster, as they neared her front door.

The two police officers stood in the doorway of the lounge and invited her to sit down, but Lucille refused, too anxious and nervous of the news to follow.

The eldest of the two police officers, took off his hat, stopped, turned to her, and took a deep breath.

"It's... it's your parents" he said, "they were found this morning, I am so sorry Lucille, but there was nothing that could have been done, from what we could make out, they would have died instantaneously from the sheer impact of the car crash, and as a result would not have suffered, or felt any pain.

The world around her seemed to halt, the plate she had been washing slipped from her hands, shattering on the floor, echoing like the sudden void in her chest. "No, no, that can't be right," said Lucille "They were both fine the last time I saw them, are you certain ?

The policeman's gaze averted to the floor, before looking directly at Lucille. "I am so sorry," he said, "but the identification that we found on the bodies, would suggest it was your parents, but obviously we will need you to formally identify them."

Her legs felt weak, the room spun, Shadows danced along the walls, and the sunlight seemed to dim. "I need… I need a moment," whispered Lucille, as she retreated to the balcony outside, the air felt heavy and thick, as if the weight of the news was pressing down on her chest.

The words were short yet final, both her parents had died in a car accident, they were both dead, and would never be coming back, Lucille would never see her beloved parents again.

Lucille slowly walked back into the lounge, the room swam into darkness and threatened the periphery of her vision, her body throbbing and pulsating as she tried not to pass out, a large stone of distress sunk into the pit of her stomach, as she choked on the bile in her mouth, she doubled over in anguish, her legs buckled from underneath her as she struggled to keep her body upright.

Lucille could hear the concerned voice of the police officer, and felt his gentle hand on her shoulder, but was unable to comprehend what she was hearing or seeing.

She tried to cry, but the sound remained cracked and caught in her throat, the screams that finally came, were ones of silent anguish as she finally passed out onto the floor.

When Lucile finally came to, one of the police officers were knelt down in front of her, "Please," said Lucille "please just go," "I just… I want to be alone.

Her voice was soft, almost fragile, as if her heart would break any minute. Lucille remained on the edge of the sofa unable to move, night came, the shadows climbed the walls, and then declined, as the sun rose.

Lucille rose slowly from where she had been sat through the entirety of the night, then in a trance-like state, she showered, got dressed, put her coat on, and headed on out.

Lucille left the brightness of the morning sun, and cautiously pushed open the door to the mortuary entrance, then made her way down a seemingly never-ending hallway, the dull beige tiles led onwards, past identical doorways edged in grey. To Lucille it seemed like one of those bad dreams, an never ending hallway, where the walls seemed to grow from the floor, and stretched upwards to the matching ceiling.

Lucille finally reached the doorway, she reached out her fingertips as if to push the door open, then paused as the morgue attendant opened the door, despite the white overall that he wore, it was evident from his haunted eyes, and wrinkled face, that he had witnessed enough morning in the tiny room she was about to enter.

Everything in the room appeared as if it had been designed to remind the visitors of the cruelty and power of death. The floor was appropriately solid concrete, rough and cold, the walls were painted a ghostly dark grey, and the ceiling loomed high and intimidating. The air conditioner whirled softly as if in silent mourning for the dead, the only bulb in the room beamed brightly to counter the gloom in the room.

Lucille shivered at the cold that seemed to be emanating from the walls. The silence was broken, as the attendant cleared his throat, and asked Lucille if she was ready, Lucille was unable to answer, but indicated a response by nodding her head, the attendant stepped forward, and very slowly pulled back the sheet that covered the body nearest to her.

Lucille drew in a sharp intake of breath and scrambled backwards, as her eyes locked onto the lifeless face of her Mother, She bit her hands, trembling, mustering everything she had inside to control herself from screaming, as the attendant uncovered the second body.

Lucille wrenched open the door, her footsteps pounding as she ran down through the hallway, her hand reaching out in desperation for the handle of the front door, collapsing into a heap onto the pavement outside. She felt the air engulf her in a warm blanket, slowly unfreezing her body from the cold, her mind unable to comprehend the horror of seeing both her parents dead, as she slowly walked back home.

For a second night in a row, Lucille was unable to sleep, with the absence of her parents her house no longer felt like a home, but a cruel reminder of the life she once had.

The weeks that passed were the most painful, Lucille had never imagined that at the age of twenty, she would be planning for her parents' funeral. The time that followed was a blur, her worn-out heart in her chest felt broken, the intense sadness was overwhelming, the feelings of unreality and disconnection remained, as she sat looking at the funeral arrangements in front of her.

Weeks later, and on a dark rainy day that matched the tear-stained faces of the mourners, Lucille watched on as they lowered the coffins of both her parents into the ground, she remained numb, no tears would come, she gripped her hands together in hope that the pain would subside if she squeezed them hard enough, but the wrenching pain remained. The emotional pain flowed out of every pore of her body, Lucille held onto her chair, so that the violent shaking would not cause her to fall, then leaned forward and picked up the two red roses, that had been laid at her feet, then threw them into the open grave, the grave was covered with soil, and flowers were laid, Lucille's gaze fell from bloom to bloom, so vibrant and full of colour, which within a few weeks, would be as dead as her parents that lay below them.

Lucille slowly and silently, walked along the winding path in the graveyard, stopping momentarily by some old and forgotten gravestones. Most of the inscriptions were unreadable, like Braille, the weather and time itself, had erased the names, dates, and kind words of remembrance. Sharp waves of pain swept through Lucille's chest, and it was then that she realized, for the first time ever, she was truly alone.

Chapter Four

Spring had finally arrived, the City had awoken from its winter slumber, bursting into a vibrant tapestry of colors and life.

The air now fragrant with the sweet scent of blooming flowers, as Lucille made her way to the theatre. The birds had returned to the trees, filling the sky with their cheerful melodies, the early morning sun shining warmly, coaxing the tender green shoots from the earth.

For many the spring brought with it a cause to celebrate, a sense of renewal, rebirth and hope, but Lucille felt nothing. In the two months that had passed, the same unyielding pain remained in her heart. The day of rehearsals had gone smoothly, but something was missing, the melody of the music failed to lift her spirits.

Lucille felt detached from the world she once loved, she felt nothing anymore, other than a sense of loss, grief and pain. The sun fell over the City, as Lucille watched on from her tiny dressing room window, as the crowds slowly made their way up the stone steps of the theatre. Lucille's heart started to race, her heart was filled with fear, she felt nauseous, she rushed to the bathroom, splashing her face with water, her heart pounding against her chest hard and loud, as she looked into the mirror, "come on," said Lucille, "come on, you can do this."

The light above the door in Lucille's dressing room illuminated, alerting her that the show was about to start, her legs shook as she made her way along the narrow corridors, now standing in the wings of the stage.

Lucille stood listening to the musicians in the orchestra, individually adjusting their instruments, practicing short scales or excerpts, to prepare for the performance of Swan lake. Normally Lucille loved to perform; dancing was where she felt most alive, but not today.

Her eyes remained shut, she could still hear the deafening thunder of her heart, as Remy the stage manager signalled for her to go on.

Lucille was numb with fear but rose out of her state of mind, transforming her body into autopilot.

Lucille stood alone on the stage, the curtains were pulled back, revealing the faces of the audience below, the music began to flitter into her ears, the jewels of her black tutu sparkling under the stage light, her foot on pointe ready for the opening scene of Swan Lake.

The fear returned at full thrust, Lucille's legs went weak, as she gasped for air under the spotlight, the emotional pain flowed out of her body, Lucille grasped her hands around her throat, as if to silence the pain, but from out of her mouth came a cry so raw, that it made it impossible to hide the anguish, as she stood exposed and alone on the stage.

A great sob escaped her lungs, as she covered her face with shaking hands, the air seemed thick with sorrow, her pain almost palpable to the onlookers. The orchestra ceased to play, silence enveloped the theatre, broken only by the sound of Lucille's sobbing uncontrollably on stage. Her eyes wide with fear and anguish, as she looked out into the shocked and saddened faces of the audience below.

Her legs trembled and her hands shook, her vision blurred, as she tried to shield her eyes from the lights that were amplifying the look of anguish on her face.

Remy ran forward grabbing furiously at the lines on the pulley to close the curtains, but the rope slipped awkwardly in his fingers. "For goodness sake," he shouted, "someone help me."

Lucille was no longer in control, She staggered backward, her mind swirling, her breaths shallow, Lucille felt the ground drop away beneath her, the cool air rushing past her face, the faces of the audience spinning wildly before her eyes. With a sickening thump, she hit the floor, the impact reverberating through her bones.

Remy let go of the rope, and rushed towards her, he knelt down on the stage and lifted Lucille into his arms, her body hanging like a damaged bird, as she was carried off the stage.

As the world around her swam into focus, Lucille blinked against the harsh light filtering through the window. The room felt foreign, the air thick with the scent of antiseptic. Her body lay heavy against the black leather of the padded bench, each breath a laborious effort.

Panic surged through her temple as fragmented memories flickered in Lucille's mind, as she willed the nausea to subside.

"Lucille? You're awake!" A familiar voice cut through the haze, and her eyes flew open again. Remy hovered over her, concern etched across his face.

"What happened?" Lucille croaked, her throat was dry, her body still shook uncontrollably. Remy protectively tucked in the blanket around her, then pulled up a chair next to her.

"You passed out," he said, "You need to take it easy Lucille." The relief washed over his face as Lucille pulled herself back up into a sitting position.

Lucille's heart raced as reality crashed back in. She had pushed herself too far, she knew she wasn't ready and now she was here, laying in the first aid room, vulnerable and exposed. A wave of shame mingled with exhaustion, as she laid back down and pulled the blanket back over herself.

"I can't keep doing this," she whispered, more to herself than to him.

Hours later, and now recovering from the ordeal, Lucille stared into the reflection of her face in her dressing room mirror.

It was in that single moment in time, that it dawned on Lucille, that she could never dance again.

Lucille recalled the words of her Mother, when she had once before wanted to give up ballet as a child, after she had fallen in front of an audience on stage. "Lucille my love," she had said, "you can't just give up just because you didn't succeed once, Just try one more performance and give it your all. I'm sure you'll want to continue after that."

But Lucille just knew it was over, as she slowly unlaced the ribbon of her shoes, the silkiness of the ribbon slipping from her fingers, as she discarded her ballet shoes on the floor.

Consumed by grief and fear, Lucille had not only lost her confidence, but the will to dance too, without her beloved parents, there seemed no point.

Lucille left silently from the side stage door, and found refuge in the quiet surroundings of a bijou backstreet café, aimlessly twirling her spoon around in her chic little cup of espresso, hoping somehow, that the tiny ripples would hold some secret clues to where her life would take her next.

Chapter Five

Lucille used to love the vibrant ambience of the city, each and every avenue was like a scene from a romantic painting, with its elegant buildings, edged by the charming street cafes, each corner unraveling a delightful surprise, a tapestry of life and culture, all rolled into one magical dream, where you could lose yourself in the ambience of the city.

She missed sitting out on the terrace leading out from their lounge with her parents, taking in the pleasant and familiar views of the city, the cars casting chromatic hues, which clashed against the beige of the city, the Eiffel Tower glittering in the background, in what had once been, their city of love and hope.

To all that travelled through Paris, they saw it for what it was, "The city of light," but to Lucille, without her beloved parents, it had become a place of despair and darkness.

The bustle of the city once enjoyed, now seemed unbelievably loud, and the grand buildings that lined the streets made her feel claustrophobic. Lucille needed to escape, she needed to find a place where she could once more feel at peace.

Lucille dreamed of a place far from the crowded streets of Paris, a place where time knew no boundaries, with wide open spaces to come up for air

She wanted to walk on faraway shores, and feel the warm loose golden sand beneath her feet, then step into the crystal cold clear waters of the sea, and float on her back, on the soft swell of the waves, her face aglow with the heat from the midday sun.

Then as this glorious day came to a close, she would sit on the beach, watching on as the moon melted into the rising tide, its luminous beams scattering tiny dancing fireflies on the surface of the water until the night reached its final act, engulfing the water under its dark cloak.

Lucille however still had an arduous few weeks of dealing with solicitors ahead of her, so was unable to make any immediate plans, until the reading of the will had taken place, but that day had finally arrived.

The soporific office was a monotonous sea of grey cubicles, with no windows, lit only by the glow of the fluorescent lights overhead, the hum enough to lull anyone to sleep.

Lucille found the environment stifling, and wished she could escape the mundane surroundings of the solicitor's office.

Lucille tried to remain calm, but the bleak surroundings did little to assist her nerves, the blood pounded in her ears, her heart thudded in her chest, as she tried to breathe.

It felt like someone was clutching her throat, and preventing her from taking full breaths of air, the tears started to trickle down her cheek, as she tried to control her breathing, she simply had to get away.

Lucille tried to stand, but her feet tingled, and her vision started to disfigure, as she fainted heavily onto the linoleum floor.

Lucille finally came round, and squinted her eyes against the shafts of daylight coming through the window, her solicitor Monsieur Dumas knelt in front of her.

"It's alright," he said, "I think you may have had a panic attack, and then passed out. I carried you into my office, where it's a bit quieter. For now, just close your eyes and concentrate on your breathing."

With Lucille so fragile, Monsieur Dumas chose a more sensitive approach that day, opting for the comfort of the old sofa in the office, where he delivered the news as sensitively as possible.

He informed Lucille that she would indeed be the sole beneficiary of all her parents' worldly goods.

This news gave her no satisfaction, and although she would be financially stable, she would swap every pound of the inheritance, in favor of her parents still being alive.

Lucille left the proceedings in the hands of the family solicitor, and then aimlessly strolled into a nearby café, and ordered a coffee.

Her attention was drawn to a magazine that had been abandoned on the table next to hers. She picked it up, nonchalantly turning the pages, and that's when she saw it, a travel piece on an island not far from France.

The writing below described it as, "An island bathed in golden sunlight, an enchanting paradise, boasting pristine white sandy beaches that stretched as far as the eye could see, fringed by lush palm trees swaying gently in the warm breeze, where crystal-clear waters lapped against the shore, beckoning visitors to immerse themselves in their refreshing embrace, offering a haven of tranquility and serenity.

Chapter Six

After a restless few weeks, Lucille's mind was made up, she packed up a few treasured items, and arranged for the remainder of her belongings to go into storage, and then made arrangements with a local rental agency to let out the flat.

For some reason she didn't want to leave it empty, it made her feel happy to think that somebody else would be enjoying her beautiful home, as her family once had, she stood in the now empty apartment, looking at a faded square about six inches above the mantelpiece where a family picture of herself and her parents once hung.

Lucille walked into the kitchen, to make sure that the boiler was turned off, it felt cold, normally it was constantly warmed by the presence of family, talking, and cooking, the kitchen floor however, had always been cold, Lucille distinctly remembered braving the frigid hardwood floor, to acquire a quick midnight snack, or to give her Mother a hug, before she left for ballet practice.

Her Father would be sitting in the designated old pine chair fiddling with the papers. Lucille switched off the water boiler, she sighed heavily, letting her head drop, before walking to the front door, and locking it.

It pained her to be leaving her home, but if, and when she was ready, she would still have a place to return to.

A week later Lucille had visited her solicitor once again, and informed him she was leaving France the following morning, but would call him once she was settled, and give him a forwarding address.

As the sun rose over Paris the next morning, Lucille checked out of the hotel she had been staying in, and made her way to the bus station, handed the driver her luggage, and found a seat in the corner on the back of the bus. It wasn't long before the bus was full of passengers, and now driving through the familiar streets of Paris, destined for the port of Saint Malo.

As they reached the boundaries of the city, Lucille looked back over her shoulder. She felt sad to be leaving, but hoped to think that wherever she travelled to, her parents would be watching over her.

It wasn't long before the bus arrived in the rolling hills of the countryside, with it's infinite variety of landscapes, vineyard-covered hillsides, charming valleys, and dense forests, then small villages, their cobblestone streets lined with pretty ivy-covered shuttered houses, intermingled with flowery squares, and bubbling fountains.

Lucille felt a sense of renewed calm as her journey continued. Her eyes grew heavy as the early morning sun filtered through the bus window.

Tired from the previous week's proceedings, she leant her shoulder against the warmth of the glass and fell into a blissful sleep.

Lucille woke just as the bus was arriving in the suburbs of St Malo, a surge of exhilaration filled her heart, with the realization that in just a few hours, the new chapter of her life would begin. Lucille collected her luggage from the bus driver, then made her way to the ferry terminal.

Lucille then bought a one-way ticket for the first ferry leaving that day, it would be a few hours before the departure, so Lucille found a comfortable spot on the harbor wall.

Lucille watched out into the distance at the comings and goings of the port. Boats bobbed and toiled against the strong offshore breeze, overhead, the cries of seagulls hung heavy in the air.

Her attentions, however, were momentarily distracted by two rather mischievous children, hurling a wooden crate into the sea. As the crate floated in on the current and came into view, much to Lucille's distress, inside, was a very small white kitten.

The poor little thing was completely drenched, its tiny cries of distress audible over the sound of the hissing sea. The kitten was now in real danger as the waves lapped over the lip of the crate. So, without a moment's hesitation, Lucille reached over the sea wall and pulled the crate, and its contents to safety.

The tiny kitten was shivering from head to tail, its fur was completely soaked, Its eyes wide with fear, trembling violently from its ordeal.

Lucille wrapped her cardigan around it, and held it close to her chest to warm up its tiny frame. After a while she could feel the shaking subside, as the kitten snuggled against her chest, the shaking now replaced by the comforting vibration of a purr.

Lucille gently pulled open her cardigan, its fur now dry revealing a coat of pure white fur that appeared soft and cloudlike; its fur was particularly fluffy around the neck and tail, with buttermilk stripes.

The kitten opened its eyes and looked at Lucille, revealing the most beautiful azure blue eyes that contrasted against the white fur, making them appear even more round and prominent. Lucille could not imagine why anyone would have tried to rid themselves of such a darling little kitten. "Well," said Lucile to the kitten, "so very pleased to make your acquaintance, and assuming you have no objections, which I imagine you don't, after nearly drowning, it looks like you and I are heading off for a new life, on the Island of Jersey."

The old wooden crate had derived from the vibrant flower markets, a place very familiar to Lucille, where she had once wandered through the Orangery style pavilions, while breathing in the sweet infusion of the powdery fresh cut flowers. The crate still retained the fragrant bouquet of lilies, so it only seemed apt that a kitten of such beauty, and one so sweet, was deserving of such a pretty name. "So" said Lucille, "It looks like fate has taken a part in giving you a name, Lily it is."

Who knew where time would take them, and what destiny had in store for Lucille and Lily, as they boarded the boat that would take them to the next chapter of their lives.

A future in limbo, now written in the stars. With Lily safely at her feet, nestled into her cardigan inside the wooden crate, there were no feelings of trepidation or fear, Lucille just knew she was sailing towards a new life of happiness. She turned for one last look, France now a distant memory on the horizon, as the ferry chugged through the dark and cold waters of the briny channel.

Lucille made her way down to the passenger lounge, and found a quiet area to sit by the window, until many hours later, with the horn on the ferry announcing its arrival to the lighthouse. Lucille stood on the deck, watching on, until the sunset came in its boldest blaze of fiery red, the sun bowed down further still, the last few lances of light casting golden fingered beams over the little harbor of St Helier, as it opened up from the sea.

Chapter Seven

The passenger ferry slowly and cautiously approached the rocky inlet, flanked by sheer and jagged cliffs, navigated safely in by the bright beacons of a nearby lighthouse.

Tiny cottages hugged the cliff edge; and was without a doubt, a sight to behold, and looked especially enchanting with the vast and resplendent castle, a bastion fortification standing strong, a protector to all that lay beneath it.

The harbor of St Helier was both beautiful and dramatic, with the valley rising steeply up on either side. The ferry sounded its horn once more to announce its arrival, before chugging up beside the old granite wall, and with the ferry now safely anchored, Lucille collected her belongings, then disembarked with her new feline companion.

With the onset of her new life before her,
Lucille took her first step onto the island of Jersey, and made her way across the cobbles of the harbor wall.

A jumble of whitewashed fisherman's cottages, set on narrow winding streets, spilled down to the harbor wall, the warm glow from the windows casting a golden path on the cobblestones as Lucille made her way along the path that curled around the bay, she arrived at the beginning of the cobbled high street, walking past the many seaside taverns, stopping momentarily to look through the tiny gift shop windows.

After such a long journey, and with a distinct lack of food on board, Lucille had grown hungry, and judging by the small cries coming from the wooden crate, so had Lily, so was enticed into a cafe that offered a delicious smorgasbord of salads and freshly caught fish.

With their bellies now full, Lucille set off to find suitable lodgings for them both, night was fast approaching, so she needed to find accommodation that would accept not just her, but Lily too.

Luckily for Lucille, there was no shortage of accommodation in St Helier, and within the hour, Lucille had found herself and Lily a darling little boarding house at the far end of the harbor, overlooking the sea.

The stone built lodging house was rustic yet charming, and still held signs of its previous grandeur with its old cast-iron balustrades, the intricate yet fragile scrolls lacked luster, with a brittle coating of flaked and reddish rust, no doubt eroded from the salty sea air.

Lucille made her way up the softly winding stairs, and opened up the door into a room, which for now, would be their temporary home, that was, until she found something more permanent.

The room was small but sufficient, the guest room exuded a faded opulence, its walls adorned with gilt-framed landscapes of a bygone era. The heavy velvet curtains that framed the shutters, once a deep burgundy, now dulled by years of sun exposure, barely held back the moonlight streaming into the room. A mahogany dresser stood against one wall, its mirror slightly tarnished but still reflecting the room's warm charm. The bed, a large double, dominated the centre, its embroidered duvet a patchwork of burgundy and gold.

A small desk was nestled in the corner, cluttered with travel books and tourist guides. The air held a faint trace of lavender from the aging potpourri on the dresser.

Lucille walked across the wooden floor, which creaked on every step, and pulled back the curtains.

 It dawned on Lucille just how quiet it was, the only sound to be heard was the sea gently lapping against the harbor wall.

Lucille looked up to the sky, which was now a velvet dark ceiling, embellished with the glitter of a million stars, it was a sight to behold, and a seemingly magical end to Lily and Lucille's first day on the beautiful island of Jersey.

After a day filled with trepidation and tired from their voyage, Lucille climbed wearily into a bed of crisp cotton sheets, and placed Lily at her side, the pair were soon enjoying the warmth from the patchwork eiderdown, as they both drifted off to the rhythmic percussion of the waves.

Chapter Eight

The sun rose with great elegance, the sky now etched with the delicate blush of salmon pinks and sanguine rose. The just-risen sun casting a vibrant glow over the new day.

Lucille awoke to the raucous sound of herring gulls, and padded gently across to the window. The sight was one of absolute joy, as fishing boats bobbed and lolled on the gentle crest of the waves.

The harbor was now a busy hive of activity. fishermen sat on the sea wall mending their nets, whilst locals emerged from their homes, exchanging pleasantries as they drifted in and out of the nearby streets. Shop shutters rattled as they were raised, and doors now open, to welcome the first customers of the day.

The inviting aroma of the salty air, which carried a heavenly scent of coffee and freshly baked bread, pervaded Lucille's nostrils. The sweet and yeasty tang from the nearby Boulangerie was enough to lure her from her room, now ready and dressed for whatever the day may bring.

Lucille headed on out of the guesthouse, leaving Lily still curled up in the folds of the soft eiderdown, and strolled very slowly along the quaint little harbor, stopping only momentarily to look back across at the channel.

Lucille finally arrived at the bakery, but was met with a scene of absolute chaos, and one very anxious proprietor doing his best to calm down the madding crowd.

The man behind the till, was tall, but heavyset, he had a round friendly face, and deep-set brown eyes, his plump cheeks were flushed, no doubt exasperated by the crowd of incredibly angry customers in his shop, he let out a slow hesitant smile as Lucille approached.

"I am terribly sorry" he said to Lucille, "I am not having the best start to my day, my son Andre was cycling into work this morning, he tried to avoid a dog, that had ran out in front of him, whilst freewheeling down one of the steep hills, he took quite a knock to the head, as he crashed head first onto the cobblestones of the street, he is at the hospital as we speak, waiting to find out if he has concussion.

"So if you are too enquiring into the whereabouts of your delivery, I must apologize, regrettably, we will be unable to fulfil any of our orders today, and for many weeks to come." With the angry crowd now spilling out onto the pavement and beyond, Lucille saw this as an opportune moment, to not only offer this poor man some assistance, but hopefully gain employment too.

"I am so terribly sorry to hear about your son," said Lucille, "and I do hope that he has not sustained any serious injuries, undoubtedly he is in the best place, and receiving the best treatment possible, I can see you are in a bit of a fix, and would be happy to help, I literally arrived on the island last night, so very much in need of a job."

Monsieur Babine, stopped and thought for a moment, he didn't know how long his son Andre would be indisposed for, and didn't want to let down his valuable customers, so Lucille's offer of help seemed like a perfect solution right now. Luckily for Lucille, Monsieur Babine, was very much in need of help, so after he had closed the shop for lunch, he met up with Lucille in the tiny back office of his shop, and gave her a very brief interview, whereby she was offered the temporary position of a delivery girl. Lucille however would need to find a suitable bike, and be at the bakery the following morning at six o'clock.

Lucille had an industrious nature, and set off immediately, searching through the endless plethora of clutter in the many bazaars, until she found a bike that was both affordable and reliable.

The bike, a Columbia Fire bolt, with a turquoise frame, a true retro classic, was just perfect for what she had in mind, including the large back bracket for the deliveries.

The best thing about the bike was the extra-large wicker basket, with two sturdy metal clips, that hooked on the front handle-bars, which would enable Lily to travel around with her.

Lucille then made her way back to the guest house, aware that Lily had been on her own for quite a while, and no doubt would be in need of some lunch.

Whilst she had been out looking for the bike, she had found a pet shop in one of the back streets of the markets, where she purchased some much needed provisions for Lily too, she had brought her a little ceramic bowl, and some mackerel from the fish market.

So for now, Lucille's future was a great deal more secure. In less than twenty four hours, she had not only found accommodation, but temporary employment too, which not only gave her precious time to find a more permanent job, but accommodation too.

The first few weeks on the island were truly enjoyable, she very much enjoyed working for Monsieur Babine, he was very easy to work for, and never minded Lily coming along.

The added bonus had to be the delicious pastries left over from the day's trading, which Monsieur Babine would leave out for her once she had returned from a day of deliveries, which Lucille more often than not, would share with Madame Elise who owned the beautiful little guest house.

Lucille simply loved traveling through the scenic back roads delivering freshly baked bread to Monsieur Babine's customers, after her delivery round was finished, she would cycle out to the north side of the island, then travel by foot down the well-worn paths, dotted with pink thrift and yellow gorse, to the sea below.

Each cove was so different, and held their own infinite charm, however Lily was not a fan of the sea, or the flint lined paths, so would opt for a shady spot on the grass, and wait for Lucille to return.

With the sun now low in the sky, Lucille cycled back to the main road, then turned off down to the winding lane which led to Plémont beach, the view was staggering as she freewheeled down the path, with Lily sat upright in the basket.

The cove was shouldered dramatically by cliffs that
sheltered and hugged the crescent shaped sweep of
golden sand that lay below it. The mighty heap of sea
flowed in its astral-blue smoothness from the horizon
into a thin seam, where the canopy of the sky, and the
plane of sea, hemmed each other into a line of silver.
Lucille spread out her cardigan on a granite rock
warmed by the sun, she lifted Lily out of the basket,
sat her on her lap, where they sat together watching
the gulls circle overhead until the sun melted into the
sea.

Chapter Nine

There was one evening that had never left Lucille's memory, it was an unusually warm evening, Lucille was sat cross-legged on the old ladder-back chair, enjoying the refreshing breeze that floated in off the sea, as she gazed out of the window taking in the view of the pretty harbor below.

Lily was curled up, sleeping soundly on the bed.
The night seemed just too beautiful to waste, so Lucille gave Lily a reassuring stroke on her head, and headed out of the door.

She cycled up to the southeast tip of the island, stopping off at La Roque Harbor, the tide was low, exposing the landscape of the jagged rocks, and deep rock pools. The scene on such a barmy night was just too inviting, so she climbed very cautiously over the rocks, and made her way down to the beach below.

She took off her sandals, and scrunched her toes into the cold wet sand, the moon dipped behind the clouds, and gradually Lucille's eyes began to adjust to the strange light around her.

The sand appeared as an eerie shade of grey, and the sea and sky an inky black, with the absence of the light of the moon.

Lucille gently swept her feet across the ground, the sand below her feet transformed into a glorious canvas of constellations. She looked up to the stars, and down to the speckled brightness on the ground below, it was a strange and otherworldly experience as she walked further down to the shoreline, and stepped into the water's edge, the sheer coldness of the sea was very welcome as the gentle waves lapped around her ankles.

It was then that the magic really happened, at first it seemed as though the stars above were reflected at her feet, but as Lucille looked closer, she could see a green bioluminescent sheen in the water, emitted by tiny glow worms. Lucille had never forgotten the true magic of that night, but at the same time, it made her feel sad to think there was no one to share it with.

Lucille was beginning to be drawn in by the magical charm of the island, and for the first time in what seemed like an eternity, she felt at peace with herself. It felt at last, like her life was turning a corner, her new life on the island was helping her to build new memories,

Lucille continued her walks along the bay, it helped her, and made her feel more present in the moment, and to enjoy the beauty of the life around her

There were times when her thoughts would wander, a sudden tooting of a car horn, or a loud bang would trigger her to relive the trauma. In these moments Lucille would search for the beauty around her, and take in deep breaths of fresh air and focus on her surroundings.

Lucille would zero in on things she could see, hear, or smell, walking on the beach barefoot, feeling the sand beneath her feet. It helped her to intensify her senses and see again how beautiful this world could be. For a few minutes, Lucille would forget about her fear, but she would never forget her parents, no matter how painful the memories were to retrieve. In time she hoped only the good memories would remain.

This new path in her life had allowed the bad memories of her past to fade, and encouraged the good memories to blossom and grow.

Chapter Ten

It was down to these very bike rides that Lily ended up having her signature pink neckerchief, fashioned from one of Lucille's old tutu's, which Lucille would pull over Lily's head to protect her delicate white ears from the scorching heat of the sun.

This silken neckerchief was a poignant symbol, not only a link from Lucille's past, but a connection to their future, a future sadly so, that would be fringed with sadness.

Lucille just loved working for Monsieur Babine, he was a very generous boss, but she was aware that Andre was now recovered, and once deemed fit by the local doctor, he would be returning back to work, so she had spent her Sunday evening trawling through the vacancies in the local paper, but it was hopeless, most of the jobs required you to have a vehicle, or at the very least know how to drive.

On Sunday evening, Monsieur Babine sat in his office, going over the monthly accounts. Trade had been great, but he simply could not afford to keep Lucille on. He had grown very fond of Lucille, but he simply had no choice, he would have to let her go.

So it was with a heavy heart that he had to deliver the news to Lucille on the Monday morning, when she had turned up for what would be her last day working as a delivery girl.

Monsieur Babine had been sitting out on the bench in front of his shop the following day, enjoying the late afternoon sun, when his dear friend, Madame Rossi had come hobbling along the street with great difficulty, she was struggling to navigate the cobbles, and very much in need of a rest.

"Please Madame Rossi," he said, "Come and sit with me on my bench, come and take the weight off your feet, you look absolutely exhausted."

Madame Rossi, held her walking stick directly in front of her, and very slowly sat down. "Oh Mr. Babine," she said, "I simply can't go on like this anymore, my poor limbs are aching, I can't keep making these trips into town, I fear I will have to move into one of those awful retirement buildings." "But Monsieur Babine," "how could I possibly leave my beautiful cottage, it holds so many dear memories to me, leaving it would break my heart."

Monsieur Babine sat and thought for a moment, then a large smile spread across his chubby face,

"Madame Rossi" he said, "I think I might just have the perfect solution for you." "I had the most wonderful young lady who had been covering in Andre's absence, she is so pleasant, and a very hard worker too, I could highly recommend her, but she does come as a pair, she has a beautiful white cat, who no doubt would be extremely helpful in keeping those mice out of your cottage."

Madame Rossi smiled, and patted Monsieur Babine's arm. "Well' she said, "It's not the worst idea I have heard, and it would allow me to stay at home. If this young lady is agreeable, please do send her up to my cottage this evening." Lucille immediately warmed to the elderly lady. She had a warm smile, dandelion-grey hair, and the darkest of eyes set back in a world-weary face.
Each wrinkle on her face told a story of struggle and survival, with the memories of the occupation and decades of history hidden within her mind.
Lucille was intrigued and heartened by this wonderful elderly lady, who had lived in the cottage for the entirety of her life, and was pretty much self-sufficient, living off the vegetables from her cottage garden, and the plentiful array of fish from the bay below.

However, the latter years had not been kind to Madame Rossi, leaving her unable to fend for herself.

Much to Lucille's delight, she was successful in the interview, and secured the position as a live-in housekeeper for Madame Rossi, and was extremely grateful to Monsieur Babine for recommending her.

Lucille had witnessed many beautiful things whilst living in Paris, but none of them compared to the beauty of the cottage.

The verdant cottage appeared as an organic extension of its vibrant surrounding, with its ivy-clad walls, and a thatched roof, that blended seamlessly with the emerald foliage, and flourishing, yet slightly overgrown living tapestry of climbing vines. It was an enchanting little haven, where the boundary of both indoors and outdoors blurred.

Lucille had really loved the first few days of living in the cottage, which was a cozy little haven, the lounge breathed punches of green and coral accents, seagrass rugs, seashells, driftwood, and bottle green glass fragments from the beach, decorated the cottage window ledges, no doubt collected by Madame Rossi, from her many trips to the beautiful beach below.

The cottage emanated a cozy and earthy charm, with its weathered wooden beams, stone fireplace, and rustic old wooden kitchen. Lucille was given the front bedroom that faced out towards the sea, and just like every other room in the cottage, it was simply decorated, yet cozy. At night time Lucille would sit on the bed that was nestled under the eaves, with Lily curled up on her lap, and watch out the window as the sunset dipped over the sea. Lucille would close her eyes and hold her face up to the golden rays of sunshine as they cast a warm yellow glow through the bedroom window.

Lucille and Lily spent many happy years in the beautiful cottage on the cliff and became the closest of friends, until Madame Rossi became too frail, and sadly so, had to move into a retirement home, whereby she left the cottage and its belongings to Lucille.

The cottage seemed lonely at first. Lucille very much missed the company of Madame Rossi, but as time passed, she enjoyed the solitary lifestyle.

Once a week she would venture into the town and visit Madame Rossi, sharing stories of the cottage and taking in fresh vegetables from the garden, which she by now, had lovingly restored to its former glory.

Lucille and Lily had adapted very easily to their life on the cliff, and she remained forever grateful to Madame Rossi for bequeathing them such a generous gift. In the summer, Lily would laze happily in a sunny spot, soaking up the cool from the old slate floor, and in the winter, curl up in front of the golden heat from the fire, nestled in her battered old wooden crate.

Their life was simple but pleasurable, a breakfast of croissants and cheese, then Lily would laze happily on the shabby patio table, scratching her claws into the now weathered and splintered wood. Lucille would make her way down the sandy footpath to the bay below, hopefully returning with a fish for both their lunches. Weather permitting, they would spend their afternoon basking in the garden under the honeyed tones of the sun.

As dusk returned, the lighthouse would once more illuminate, casting narrowed sweeping beams of light over the tiny cottage.

Night-time was always Lily's favorite part of the day, when she cuddled down into the warmth of the feather duvet, Lucille would wind up the clockwork mechanism of her jewelry box, as she and Lily both drifted off to the gentle chimes of Clair de lune.

Chapter Eleven

Lucile and Lily were awoken the next morning by a steady offshore breeze. Lily sat and watched the clouds build, by now, a gale was emerging, singing through the trees, sending loose leaves dancing hypnotically to the floor.

A storm was building, black clouds danced across the sky, twisting like ballet dancers, dressed in windswept grey lace, against a stage of sepia curtains. Lucile and Lily however, had become hardened to the years of fickle island weather.

So, just like every other day, Lucille with her head down, struggled against the wind, and made her way down through the winding cliff path, whilst Lily remained safely huddled between the terracotta pots in their garden.

Little did Lucille know, but their idyllic lifestyle was in jeopardy, and this would be the last time she would see her beloved lily for many years to come.

Some might say that everything happens for a reason, and that fate has complete control of our destiny, and that we can affect our fate by the choices we make. But sadly so for Lucille, she had already chosen hers by leaving their cottage that day.

Lucille reached the beach, and with her head down against the strength of the wind, made her way to the shoreline, she held the line of the fishing rod tightly between her fingers, and fed the bait onto the hook. She shivered as the sky above filled with tumultuous dark ragged clouds, the thunder roared up above her, the storm increasing with strength as great bolts of lightning flashed across the sky.

Lucille had not realized the full extent of the storm, and felt that it was wise to return, but it was too late. The merciless wind roared across theMl , angry waves curled upwards crashing and pounding onto the beach.

Lucille saw the large wave come crashing towards her, she tried to run, but stumbled, she dropped the fishing rod from her hands, and started to crawl on all fours up the first ridge of stones, but the sheer force of the sea churned up the pebbles, dragging them and Lucille backwards into the sea.

Lucille tried to push herself out of the water, but her small frame was no match for the rough and turbulent waves that dragged her down with force; she tried to resist, flailing her arms, and frantically kicking her legs.

Fear gripped her, as she surfaced momentarily, gasping in urgent mouthfuls of air, before another large wave punched into her body, dragging her further down below, filling her lungs with icy cold water.

The minutes seemed like hours as Lucille continued to fight, the sea coming at her like a ferocious monster, trapping her in its watery white jaws, with Lucille fighting frantically to release herself from its cold clutches.

Lucille was growing incredibly weak, for over an hour she had struggled to stay afloat, as the waves crashed over the top of her, choking repeatedly on the salty water, aware that very soon, the sea would become her very own watery grave. She raised her arm upwards, as if to reach up to the sky above for help, before finally giving up and letting go, her arms fell to her side, as she sank below the surface, the blood pounding behind her eyes as she sank deeper still. There was an eerie silence after the noise of the storm that had been raging above, Lucille held her breath involuntarily, and her airway closed, as the water started to slowly fill her lungs.

Lucille blinked her eyes against the darkness of the sea, a look of bewilderment, as a ghostly white light spread on the surface of the water. Lucille was unable to comprehend what was happening at first, until she felt a hand pulling against her arm, and then another, as she was wrenched upwards over the side of a boat, and laid down on the deck.

The boat rocked violently from side to side, as the fisherman gripped onto the edge of the boat, letting go momentarily, as he forced his hands downwards onto Lucille's chest, until she gave out a labored gasp, choking with force as the sea water left her lungs.

The fisherman pushed her up into a sitting position, then pulled her arms through a life jacket. "Hang on," he shouted to Lucille, "we are not out of the worst of it yet," he then held her gaze for a second, before hurriedly returning back to the wheel house.

The captain pulled the handset from the dashboard, and uttered the words, he hoped he would never have to say, "Mayday, Mayday, Mayday, this is the captain of the fishing boat, the "Aida May."

The captain then gave them the last known position, put back the radio, he had little hope of assistance with the storm raging, but continued to battle and hold the ship steady in the raging sea.

Lucille looked up to the sky above, smoky clouds rolled in like boulders, ready to crush anything in their way. The thunder roared, the streaky lightning flashed across the sky, illuminating the dark waves whipped by the howling gale, as they rose high up above the boat, ready to charge once again at the small vessel.

The wind was icy and withering, Lucille bowed her head against the gusting wind, shivering violently as the cold waves lashed against her.

The boat heaved and tossed in the rising swell. Lucille watched on as the fisherman who had saved her, gripped the wheel with his bare hands, the waves and heavy rain combined, lashed at the side of the boat, which keeled and tilted.

The lighting above cracked and forked, hitting the boom, which exploded releasing it from the metal cables above, Lucille did not see the boom as it came crashing down, and had no time to escape, as it came falling down on top of her, knocking her into a state of unconsciousness.

The storm had not finished with them yet, increasing in strength as the waves now crashed over the bow, water gushed across the deck, drenching the crew.

The bowsprit plowed through the waves, diving under every crest. Eight-foot swells rocked the boat with an immense power that only Mother Nature could provide. Beating upwind, the boat ripped across the stormy grey ocean. Fighting through the squall at fifteen knots.

The adrenaline on board was palpable. The fear in the captain's eyes now obvious, as he struggled to regain control.

The storm inhaled, then with one mighty gasp, pulled the towering waves higher and higher, the captain looked on in horror, as the mountainous wave rose up before the wheelhouse, blotting out the sky, which released, and then came charging down on the small vessel.

The Captain shouted to the crew to hold on, but the deafening thunder drowned out his cries, as the thunderous weight of the wave hit the deck with immense force.

The wave smashed the boat into splinters, then swallowed it down into its dark abyss, spitting out the debris of the planks onto the surface, which crashed and cracked against the rocks of the shore.

The storm had finally subsided, the mighty waves, now calm, rippling against the rock, rising and falling, revealing the battered body of Lucille, her hair matted with the blood that had ran freely from the deep cut in her forehead

The left side of her face was swollen, making her eye barely open, she leaned against the cold rocks, her breathing coming in ragged gasps, each inhale a reminder of the blows her body had taken, as the sea had tossed her against the rocks. Yet, beneath the pain, a stubborn fire burned in her heart, she would not let this defeat her. Her body twitched, barely moving, the violet bruises on her arms and hands, stark against her skin, yet her shaking fingers remained, as she gripped them around the rusty chain secured to the rock.

Lucille was too weak to pull herself out onto the safety of the cobb that lay below the lighthouse, but she was not ready to give up yet.

Chapter Twelve

The next morning, Francois the lighthouse keeper, stood in the glassed-in housing at the top of a lighthouse tower, before making his way down the metal spiral staircase into the watch room, he raised the binoculars to his face, gazing out at the slothful sea, ebbing ever so gently, onto the shore below, for now, all was calm, and a stark contrast to the storm that had battered against the walls of the lighthouse throughout the night.

The coastguard had launched a lifeboat, after receiving a distress call from the Aida May, which was heading to the last known position of the fishing boat.

It was a tense and worrying time for the families waiting for news of the six crew members, who had been on board the "Aida May." For hours the lifeboat searched, but the same dark clouds threatened the sky, the ferocious wind returned as they neared the rocks that lay below the lighthouse.

The Coxswain shouted the alarm, at the sight of what appeared to be a lifeless body. It was a difficult approach, with the lifeboat itself at risk, as the swell of the waves pushed them alarmingly close to the jagged rocks.

The crew had practiced the maneuver many times, and as a result were able to reach the body of the woman, and carried her very carefully into the cabin below. The lifeboat crew could not believe it when they discovered that the woman was still alive, not only was she carrying the most horrendous injuries, but she had survived the extreme cold temperatures of the sea overnight. On examination her heart rate was dangerously low, and her breathing was shallow, she tried to open her eyes, but lost consciousness.

The captain of the lifeboat pushed the throttle forward, aware that time was not on their side, with the injuries the woman had sustained, along with the severe hypothermia, he didn't believe that she would make it, and would cease to exist, long before they reached the safety of the lifeboat house.

The ambulance was ready and waiting at the top of the slipway as the lifeboat pulled into the harbor of St Helier. Lucille's body was transferred onto a stretcher, with four of the lifeboat crew each taking a corner, as they carried her slowly and cautiously over the wet cobbles towards the ambulance.

Once safely onboard, the driver switched on the blue flashing lights and sirens on the ambulance, as they drove with urgency towards the hospital. For many days that followed, the lifeboat continued to search for the crew of the "Aida May," they did not expect to find any of them alive, but for the sake of their families, wanted to bring them home, so that they could receive a proper burial. The search however was in vain, the "Aida May," along with her crew, remained lost. On the following Sunday, the residents of St Helier, along with the families, who had lost their loved ones, stood on the harbor wall.

Rosalie stepped forward, and knelt down onto the hard stone pebbles of the sea wall, and threw a single deep red rose onto the surface of the sea, and bid a sad farewell, to her Husband, who had no doubt fought the fight of his life as the Captain of the "Aida May.

Chapter Thirteen

Lily was awoken by the rumble of thunder, Lightning cracked, forks pierced through the graphite sky, streaks of bold light illuminating the fury of the ferocious storm.

Lily curled into a tighter ball under the Laurel bush, shivering against the coldness of the night. Her tiny body was drenched from the torrential rain, trembling as each bolt of thunder exploded, watching on for what seemed like an eternity. The merciless wind remained, forcing everything out of its way, as the thick opaque clouds gathered, but one single blinding white light from the lighthouse cut through, and reminded Lily that she wasn't alone.

Lily cried out into the wind, but there was no one to hear her pitiful cries, as she climbed back under the Laurel bush, waiting for her beloved Lucille to come home.

Dawn broke with a freshness to the air. The storm had subsided. Lily arched her back, stretched, yawned, and made her way to the front door, but it remained closed, and still no sign of Lucille.

Lily, not knowing anything else other than her normal routine, resumed her position on the old patio table, waiting for the return of Lucille, not for one moment taking her eyes off the cliff path. As dusk returned, so did the same threatening clouds and torrential rain, Lily took refuge once again, under the hedge. Her little tummy was hollow, and It was increasingly hard to sleep out in the elements with the weather so bad, but more so, a deep sadness had filled her heart. Why had Lucille abandoned her, had she done something wrong?

It was days later, when the storm had finally subsided, that it dawned on Lily that she had to do something. She had to find Lucille, she had to find food. She was growing weaker with every day that passed, and knew if she waited any longer, she would not make it down to the long and rocky cliff path below.

Lily had never ventured down the steep cliff path, or ever had to fend for herself. Her beloved Lucille had always taken care of her, and in return, Lily had given her companionship and love.

Lily navigated her way down through the path, the brambles and flint stones piercing the soft pads of her feet, but yet she continued, until many hours later, when she finally reached the tiny cove.

The spume of the white capped waves rolled magnificently on the horizon, then gently crawled on the shore, trickling through the pebbles, then bubbled and hissed as it withdrew.

Lily was temporarily mesmerized by the tranquil movement of the waves, but nonetheless she kept at a safe distance from the sea, as she made her way across the hard cold pebbles which slipped and wobbled underfoot.

For weeks, Lily ambled her way through the long stretch of the island coast, stopping only to rest for minutes, taking shelter against the rocks, warmed by the midday sun.

But after weeks of searching, she was steadily growing weaker, she felt unable to take one more step, the pain was unimaginable as she placed her cracked and bleeding pads of her feet onto the hard pebbles.

she now walked with a stiffness, her tiny body was withered, her beautiful cream coat dull and unwashed.

She felt her body weaken from beneath her, but then noticed a woman, "Could this be her beloved Lucille." With every last ounce of energy, Lily forced her body into a slow run, but after weeks of hunger, in search of her beloved Lucille, her little body surrendered as she silently toppled onto the hard cold stones, the sight of the woman dimmed then disappeared as her eyelids slowly closed.

Luckily for Lily, she had indeed seen a woman in the distance, who discovered her body a while later whilst beachcombing for coastal treasures, she had cried out in alarm when she had discovered the battered body of the cat.

She knelt down in front of its tiny frame, and was astonished to see its chest slowly rising and falling in a labored motion.

She held the cat against her chest, and ran along the pebbles until she reached the car park. Once she had reached her own car, she very gently laid the cat down on the passenger seat.

Her right hand remained gripped on the steering wheel, but very gently placed her left hand on the cat, not only to reassure it if her presence, but to check that it was still breathing, as she tore off through the country lanes

Within minutes she had reached the vets, Valerie very carefully lifted up the cat from the front seat, it was still breathing, she ran into the reception room, and alerted the staff of the emergency, then sat down in the waiting room, very gently stroking the soft fur on the cat's head. "It's all right'" said Valerie to the cat ,

"Just hang in there, you are going to be ok, not long now and the vet will be free. "Monsieur Le Dieu was an exceptionally talented vet, but he feared the worst, the cat was in a bad way, suffering from malnutrition and dehydration, her paws were torn and bruised, her tiny body had endured so much.

Chapter Fourteen

The lady who had discovered Lily, was a seamstress who owned a tiny shop behind De Grucy's department store, and as soon as she had closed her shop, at the end of every day, Valerie Bisson, would travel down to the vets, she would stay for hours, gently stroking the cat. But the cat remained very poorly, and her eyes remained firmly shut.

It seemed however, that the care of Monsieur Le Dieu, along with Valerie's visits, had finally pulled Lily through. Valerie had arrived just like every other night, and was met by Monsieur Le
Dieu racing down the path of his garden.
"Valerie." he shouted, "come quickly, she is starting to come around." Valerie rushed into the lounge where the cat had been placed into a cardboard box in front of the fire, she knelt on the hearth,

and watched and waited, at first the cat's paw just twitched, but then she uncurled her paw, and for the first time since being at the vets, she opened her eyes.

Valerie gasped, she had never seen a cat with such amazing eyes, the darling little creature blinked its azure blue eyes, looking long and hard into Valerie's face, she had a pink fabric neckerchief around her neck, which was very dirty and tatty, Valerie stretched out her hand, and untied it.

"I will take this home, and wash it," she said, "We can't have a cat as glamorous as you, wearing something as scruffy and dirty as this."

Valerie went to pat the soft fur on her head, but the cat pulled away from her reach, and turned its back on her, then curled up into a tiny protective ball. Lily's eyes remained open, watching the flames dancing in the fireplace, it made her think of home, where she would be curled up In front of her own fire in her wooden crate, with Lucille sat next to her, in her battered old fireside chair.

Lily let out a little sigh, and wondered with a deep sadness, why had her dear friend not come to collect her, she simply had to leave, she needed to find Lucille.
Lily tried to stand, but she was still too weak, she tried to climb over the sides of the cardboard box, but her little legs would not work, the stiff bandages around her legs made it impossible for them to bend, so instead she gave way to the tiredness, tucked her chin into her chest, and fell asleep.

Valerie walked out of the vets, the tiny neckerchief held loosely between her fingers, but as she neared the driver's door, and pulled out the keys from her handbag, she lost her grip on the neckerchief, it dropped onto the floor, Valerie quickly bent down to retrieve it, but as she did, a gust of wind picked it up, Valerie reached up and tried to catch it, but it floated upwards into the sky, before it finally disappeared out of sight.

After a few weeks, Lily was nursed back to a stable condition, and was deemed fit enough to leave, Valerie had already agreed to take the cat, that was until her owner was found, so after she had closed her shop that day, she drove round to the vets to collect her.

 She very carefully placed the box in the front seat of her car, and stroked the cat's head, "It's alright," she said, "you are coming home with me, that is, until we find your owner."

Lily was hysterical, she had never been in a car before, and was completely panicked. Where was this person taking her, she had to get out, she simply had to find her beloved Lucille. Lily yowled and cried, she scratched at the cardboard and tried to get out of the box, but the lid had now been firmly closed, so she crouched into the corner of the box, and lowered her head.

Valerie pulled up outside her shop, which stood at the end of a charming little cobbled street, lined with decadent boutiques and table side cafes, she got out of the car, and placed the box on the bonnet whilst she unlocked the front door, then carried it into her house.

Once she had closed the front door, she opened the lid of the box, and reached inside it to lift Lily carefully out, but Lily was having none of it, she cowered into the corner of the box, her eyes darting from left to right, looking for a means of escape. "Oh you poor little thing," said Valerie, "you must be terrified, it's ok, I am going to leave the lid of the box open, you come out when you're ready."

Valerie went into her kitchen, and got two saucers out of her cupboard, she filled one with water, and chopped up a large piece of mackerel, and placed them down next to the box where the cat was sleeping. Lily however, did not come out of the box, or eat the fresh mackerel that Valerie had prepared for her, she remained inside, too scared to come out. And that is where she remained, as Valerie looked in on her just before she made her way up the stairs.

"Goodnight," she said to Lily, "Sweet dreams, you dear little cat, I will leave my bedroom door open, in case you decide to come in." But Lily did not, she stayed in the box, scared and alone, wishing more than ever for the return of her darling Lucile.

Chapter Fifteen

Valerie came down the next morning, and found Lily still cowering in the corner of the box, and the food untouched, Valerie tried yet again to pat her, but her little body stiffened at her touch.

Valerie went into her sewing room, and started rummaging through the off cuts in her drawer, she pulled out a remnant of the softest pink silk, and started up her sewing machine.

Valerie walked back into the lounge, and very gently lifted Lily out of the box, and sat her down on her lap, and patted the soft fur between her ears.

"Look," she said to Lily, "I have made you a new neckerchief, it's by no means as special as your old one, but I felt so dreadfully sorry for losing yours."

Valerie pulled the soft silk fabric around her neck, and tied it into a bow. "There," she said, "don't you look utterly beautiful."

The cat looked at her with the same empty eyes, then jumped off her lap, and padded across the floor, opting for a seat on the windowsill of the shop.

Valerie sighed, and went back into her sewing room, coming out a few hours later to check on her, the poor little cat was still sitting in the window, her eyes were wide, not for one moment averting her gaze.

So, for now, this was Lily's new home, and although she was extremely grateful for being rescued, she pined for her beloved Lucille, every day she sat in the window, watching and waiting, but with every day that passed, came the same feeling of despair.

Her beloved Lucille remained absent, but Lily would not give up, somewhere out there, was her dearest friend, and she was determined to find her.

Lilly's physical health continued to decline, with her rarely eating, and regardless of Valerie's attempts, she remained inconsolable and lifeless, her once beautiful soft coat was once again, unkempt and matted.

She refused the attention of Madame Bisson, and spent every day curled up in the shop window, watching and waiting for the return of Lucille.

Try as she might, Valerie could not lift the spirits of this dear little cat. Eventually, she had to accept defeat, and watched on every day, as Lily lay listless in the draughty shop window, a deep sadness remained in her beautiful blue eyes

Two weeks had passed, Valerie sat at the table, drinking her early morning coffee, she wiped away a tear, as she watched on, the poor little cat struggled to walk towards the window, her tiny frame was becoming alarmingly fragile.

Her steps had become increasingly slow, as she wobbled unsteadily on her feet, now unable to climb onto the shallow ledge of the windowsill. Valerie lifted her up, and seated her down gently, "There you are," she said, "Who knows, maybe today will be the day, don't lose faith my dear one."

Valerie was becoming incredibly concerned, she could feel the back bones of her spine, and she knew that if this continued, this dear little cat would not survive, and fade away to nothing.

Fearing the worst, and determined to help her, she closed the shop, and drove to the vets. Monsieur Le Dieu was as helpful as always and gave her a food supplement, which would hopefully give her cat an appetite again, and encourage her to eat.

Thankfully, it worked, at first the cat was adverse, but then gradually, she would lick the food from a teaspoon, then before long, she got her appetite back, her tiny frame filled out, but still the daily routine continued.

Lily remained in the window, a look of hope momentarily appeared as footsteps approached, which soon declined with it only being the arrival of one of Valerie's regular customers. The months passed by, and then years, and then on one particular

Sunday, Lily woke, stretched, arched her back, then padded into the room, where Valerie was busy adjusting a dinner jacket, for her most distinguished customer, the Earl of Jersey.

With a little sigh, Lily curled up onto a huge pile of leftover fabrics, and for the first time in years, curled up into a tight little ball, and fell sound asleep, purring along methodically to the sound of the sewing machine.

Lily had finally accepted that Lucille was never coming back, she didn't know what she had done wrong, or why Lucille had abandoned her, but at least she was safe and warm, and had found someone who seemed to really care for her.

Lily and Valerie enjoyed years of companionship, and although Lily had finally accepted that her beloved Lucille was gone, she was never truly the same. She would still dream of Lucille and their beautiful little cottage on the cliffs.

Valerie never did give her a name, it just didn't seem right, instead she reverted to referring to her as "Dearie," which the cat seemed to respond to.

Chapter Sixteen

By now, Lily had become accustomed to her new life in the shop, but the memory of near starvation, and searching for weeks for Lucille, along with her loss, had stayed with her.

She insisted on travelling everywhere with Valerie, fearful that she may not return, and once more she would be abandoned and alone.

On a bright and glorious morning in June, Valerie set off to her first job of the day, to a beautiful old institute, on the Trinity side of the island, it was a decadent old Manor, now called "Star Point," which had been kindly bequeathed to the islanders by the late "Madame Elise," which was now a home to those who had fallen on hard times, or struggled to deal with the constraints of everyday life.

As always, Lily travelled along in the front passenger seat of Valerie's old car, they bumped along through the winding Jersey back roads, with Valerie singing along to the radio, occasionally glancing over to smile at Lily.

They arrived at the old cast iron gates of the Manor, driving down a road arched with old Oak trees, before reaching a great sweeping driveway that took you through the most fragrant landscaped gardens. Raymond the gardener was trimming one of the many rose bushes, he tipped his cap with his thumb as Valerie drove past.

Then Valerie, with her measuring tape pad and pencil, made her way through the elaborate entrance hall, with Lily walking behind, and then into the decadent lounge, where she then started the arduous task of measuring up for what would be a set of elegant fleur-de-lis curtains.

Lily was particularly unhelpful, pawing at the measuring tape as it coiled down the grand sash windows of the lounge. Valerie smiled on as Lily played, she did not mind the interruption, and it warmed her heart to see her so happy and content.

In the corner of the lounge, one of the residents sat with her back to Valerie, gazing vacantly, smiling silently, poised as if watching a silent scene unfold in front of her, whilst her fingers tapped rhythmically on the side of the chair, whilst she held a bone china cup in the other.

Valerie hummed as she worked, smiling at the sight of Lily, bathing in the midday sun, her tiny face tilted toward the beams of light that danced rhythmically through the delicate floral patterns in the lace curtains. Her whiskers twitching, dreaming of memories gone, but not forgotten.

They were both disturbed by the shatter of china on the parquet floor. As Valerie turned, the resident now faced them, her large shallow eyes captivated at the sight of Lily.

It was then that Valerie took an intake of breath at the sight of the tiny pink silken handkerchief, neatly tucked in the cuff of her blouse, as Lily very slowly approached, now within arm's reach of the resident, she remained completely entranced. Her nose tilted upward, as if she had discovered a familiar scent, her tiny head turned, and looked back at Valerie, as if she was trying to absorb and understand what she was actually seeing in front of her.

Valerie choked back a tear as she watched Lily rubbing the side of her head against the ladies' legs, her purr loud enough to be heard from where Valerie was standing.

When the lady failed to respond, Lily started to let out the most pitiful cries. Valerie couldn't bear to hear her so upset, but just as she had reached them both, the lady scooped Lily up into her arms.

The lady searched deeply into the dark pools of her azure blue eyes.

Everything stopped existing, time held no significance. The lady frowned, a look of helpless frustration crossed her face.

The grandfather clock chimed the arrival of the hour, time resumed, and the lady placed Lily back onto the floor, and walked off into the shadows of the hall, briefly stopping to turn her head to look at both Lily and Valerie, she tried to speak, but no words would come. The look of love said it all, this was her cat, Valerie was sure.

Lily remained motionless on the floor before hurriedly running in the direction of where Lucille had left. But she was gone. "Come on," said Valerie. "Let's get you back home."

Valerie collected her belongings and scooped Lily up onto her shoulders. Lily still held her gaze into the hallway, both heartbroken and confused. Why had her beloved Lucille not recognized her, clearly, she did not love her anymore.

Chapter Seventeen

The woman stood in her room, staring vacantly out over the lawn. She watched on with interest at the woman she had just seen not moments before, gently placing her cat in the car, and then pulled the pink neckerchief over its head.

A flash of light interrupted her thoughts, then a sudden and vicious glimpse into a past no longer living; she felt a strangled choke rise to the back of her throat, and she closed her eyes to the all-encompassing feeling of darkness as it encapsulated her mind, as she was pulled back, once more into the cold and raging sea.

Her hands rose to her throat, she gasped to breathe, but then a silence, a dull buzz filled her mind, then slowly left like a gentle tide pulling away from the shore.

She straightened her body, rested one hand against the glass of the window, and drew in a great shuddering breath, the warmth of the glass bringing back a flood of memories. Tiny snippets of her past played through her brain, flicking back and forth like the reel of an old movie, Lucille opened her eyes, and looked out of the window, and that's when she saw her, and every memory came flooding back.

She banged loudly on the window, Sobbing uncontrollably, but still no words would come, they couldn't hear her. Her legs still shook from underneath her, but she willed them to move, tripping and falling as she tore across her bedroom floor, then into the hallway. She had to stop them, she had to reach them. But as she neared the front door, the car pulled away and drove steadily back down the driveway.

Now back out in the sunlight of the garden, Valerie placed Lily in the front of the car, with the scorching sun now high in the sky, she pulled the pink neckerchief protectively over Lily's head, she then busied herself putting her belongings away in the boot of the car, then climbed back into the driving seat, started the engine, and drove off down the driveway.

As Valerie neared the cast iron gates, she was momentarily distracted. As she checked the mirror of the car, she saw the same resident from moments before, running down the road behind her, waving her arms in frustration. The poor lady seemed so distressed, Valerie wondered if she should pull over, but then saw one of the nurses running behind her, so continued down the winding path of the drive, then back out onto the main road.

It was painful to see the poor woman like this. All the nurse could do was embrace her, and let the torrent of her tears soak through her blouse. She could feel her clench her fists, not knowing whether she was angry or just had given up hope altogether. She could hear the vibration, her silently screaming, suffocating with each breath she took. The nurse ran her fingers through her hair, time and time again, in an attempt to calm the silent war within her mind, as the doctor approached, the needle in his hand primed and ready to calm her down.

Lucille loosened her grip on the nurse, holding her hands up in retaliation, she had to get away, she had to find Lily. Lucille sprang up, desperate to make herself heard, indicating with her hands for a paper and pen.

Now back indoors, Lucille sat at a desk writing on the pad In front of her, as the tears flooded freely down her cheeks, she tore off a piece of paper and slid it across the desk to the nurse. Lucille jabbed her finger repeatedly on the piece of paper, a pleading look on her face, as the nurse put on her glasses. The nurse finished reading, took off her glasses, and took Lucille's hands in hers. "ok" she said, "We will take you into town, and go to the tailor shop and talk to the owner, but not now, it's too late, and you are very upset, we will go in the morning."

Lily finished her breakfast, then padded over to the window and found a warm spot where the sun was already flooding through the glass. Once settled she washed in her same meticulous and meditative way, then curled her body up, soaking up the warmth from the early morning sun.

Valerie unlocked the front door of the shop, grabbed her coffee from the kitchen, sat down at her sewing machine, pulling the heavy fabric through, as the sewing machine whirled into action.

The bell on the shop door chimed as the door opened, Lily remained asleep, after years of living in the shop, the sound of the bell had become familiar, so she remained in her comfortable spot. Valerie looked up, it was unusual to get customers so early, she put down her fabric, and made her way into the front of the shop.

Valerie was taken back, not only was the same lady from yesterday in her shop, but a nurse too. The lady very slowly walked towards where Lily was sleeping, then very gently scooped her up into her arms.

For the first time in years, Lucille breathed out her first words. It was barely audible, but clear nonetheless. "Lily," she said, "I found you."

And then, as if dancing to a silent symphony, whispering into her ears, Lucille raised Lily into the air, and with ethereal quality, moved with such passion and fluidity, it was like she was speaking and dancing from the very depths of her soul, as she twirled Lily around in the air, before finally pulling her into her chest.

Lucille fell to her knees, and hugged Lily tighter still, she was shaking and sobbing uncontrollably, she cried for the missed times they would never make back, whilst looking down at Lily, as if she were still part of a forgotten dream.

Valerie very slowly edged forward, wrapped her arms around them both, and led Lucille back into the shop.

It was undoubtedly a very emotional afternoon, but a happy one nonetheless, and although Valerie knew her time with Lily would soon end, her heart was filled with joy, fate had played a kind hand, no amount of time or space could ever separate Lily and Lucille, they were meant to spend the rest of their lives together.

The nurse went on to explain the circumstances that had brought Lucille to the home. It appeared that she had been found by the Saint Helier lifeboat crew, Lucille had sustained huge injuries, and although she recovered from the physical scars, she had never uttered a single word since arriving.

The staff had asked her on many occasions if she had a family member to contact, and offered her a pad and pencil to write, but Lucille was never able to offer any answers, and would retreat to the safety of her room.

After months of rehabilitation, with Lily allowed to visit once a week, Lucille and Lily returned once more to their darling little cottage on the Cliffs.

Chapter Eighteen

Obviously, quite a few repairs were needed after the cottage had remained empty for so long, but the first addition was a cat flap for Lily, so she would never once again, be subjected to the ever-changing Island weather.

Lucille had quite a lot of catching up to do, after remaining absent from the world for so long, but the one thing that had plagued her mind in the weeks that followed, was what had happened to the brave fisherman who had pulled her to safety on that fateful night.

The Doctor had advised her to take it slow, but she wanted to find him, and thank him for his bravery.

She travelled down to the harbor of Saint Helier, to make some enquiries, quite a few changes had taken place, but it was still the same beautiful harbor that had welcomed her on her first day, when she arrived on the island of Jersey.

She neared the busy port, watching the fishing boats bob and toil, on the waves, before making her way towards the harbor master's cottage.

The Harbor master sat outside, in deep conversation with a group of fishermen. "Excuse me." said Lucille, "I am trying to find the whereabouts of one of the captains from the local trawling boats that are moored here, It is really quite important that I find

him," said Lucille. "I Unfortunately had been suffering from amnesia, and only very recently recovered, the Captain of the ship will be wondering no doubt, why I never took the time to seek him out, and thank him for saving my life, for if it was not for the bravery of this man, I would not be standing here with you today."

The harbor master invited Lucille into his office, and that's when she saw the picture on the wall, her blood ran cold, she swayed on her feet, as she looked into the face of the person who had rescued her from the raging sea on the night of the storm.

The Harbor master pressed Lucille gently down onto the chair behind his desk, he took the picture off the wall, and placed it into her hands. "Tell me" he said, "What is it about this picture that has upset you so much?" With a shaking hand, Lucille pointed her finger towards the face of the man in the center of the picture, who had pulled her from the sea.

In a near whisper she replied, "This man, this man here, "he saved my life, he pulled me from the sea, I came to thank him, but it appears that I will never be given the opportunity."

The skin on the harbor master's face paled, his hands shook, as he retrieved a handkerchief from his trouser pocket, dabbing at his eyes until the tears gave way, running freely down his face.

"This man" he said, pointing to the picture, "was my Son Josh, I have spent the last few years wondering what became of him."

"There isn't a day that goes by where I do not wonder what happened, I begged him not to go out that night, I could see the large swells in the sea, and the threatening clouds gathering overhead, but he wouldn't listen.

I blame myself, I should have tried harder, I should have stopped him from leaving the harbor, but he just wouldn't listen."

Chapter Nineteen

The Harbor master put down the picture, and clasped Lucille's hands in between his, and then looked directly into her eyes. "Please," he said, "Will you come with me? His widow, Rosalie, lives just a few minutes away. Please, will you come with me and talk to her, you were probably the last person to see Josh alive.

"The Harbor master stood on the doorstep of the pretty fisherman's cottage with Lucille, and pushed open the door, a young woman was sat on the floor, a young child was seated on her lap as they read a book together .

"Hello Rosalie " he said, "this is Lucille and this will no doubt come as a shock, but we need to talk to you, she was rescued by your Josh on the night of the storm all those years ago, he saved her life Rosalie." "Please," he said, "can we come in." Rosalie sat for a while, just staring at them both, no doubt trying to comprehend what her Father in law had just told her, she slowly lifted the small child from her lap, stood up, and walked towards Lucille. "Come in," she said, "come and sit down, please tell me what happened to my beloved Josh."

Lucille spent the afternoon explaining to Rosalie, how very brave her late husband had been, how he had saved her life, and fought to keep the fishing boat afloat in the storm that night, she explained in great detail where the boat had been when she had been pulled on board from the raging sea. Rosalie was aware she would never truly be able to visit him, and kneel in front of his grave and lay flowers at the foot of his headstone, but it gave Rosalie a sense of comfort in knowing that his final place of rest was close by, and was not one of darkness, but illuminated forevermore, by the lighthouse standing protectively on the cliffs above.

It was yet again a very emotional day for Lucille. She felt sad that Josh, along with his crew, had not made it back through the storm, but she hoped that her speaking to Rosalie would have given her the closure she was looking for, after many years of worrying, with the knowledge that he was close by to the home that they had once shared, as Husband and Wife.

Chapter Twenty

With time, Lucille continued to recover, but the most recent events along with the death of both of her parents all those years ago, took her back to the familiar dark places that had haunted her in Paris, it made her question, "what did I ever do to deserve this, and will life ever play a fair hand, and let me find happiness."

It was then she remembered something that her Father had said to her all those years ago. "Leaving the past behind is something that many of us are afraid to do, holding on to people, places and things that are familiar often becomes a place of comfort, and inhibits your ability to grow, and chase your true dreams, there's comfort in pain, comfort in reliving something that tried to destroy you, and chase you down." "But the lesson is done," he would say, "the past cannot be changed, now let it go, and I promise that once you release everything that is holding you back, it will feel like the weight has been lifted off your shoulders and a new life will begin."

A smile flickered across her face, and it dawned on

Lucille, that her Father may not have been there in the physical sense guiding her on, but these same words had unconsciously driven her forward.

It was these words that had enabled her to let go of her past, and bravely find a new life on the island of Jersey.

Lucille realized that she had taken the harsh and painful memories from the past, and created a stronger present, and yes, undoubtedly there would be ups and downs in life, but life is life, and no matter what, giving up on your dreams and aspirations, because of a few bumps in the road, would never be an option.

She would continue to live her life, and not just for herself, but for those too who no longer were part of this world, because she would never forget them, and remember her parents always, with a fond heart.

The following month Lucille donated all of the money left to her in the will to "Star Point," so they could continue to look after those that needed it.

As for Valerie, it was either the otherworldly essence of the island that changed her path, or just karma repaying her for her kind act, but she later married a handsome fisherman, where they lived a happy and fulfilling life, in a beautiful stone cottage, nestled into the Lyme rocks of the sea wall, and call it chance, but it was aptly named, "The cat's whiskers."

Every Sunday Valerie would sail to the south side of the island, and join Lucille and Lily for a hearty lunch of fish pie, and oven baked Jersey royals, soaked in delicious black bean butter.

Lily as always would be soundly asleep on her favorite wall in the garden, bathing in the sunshine.

Lily was forever happy to be back with her beloved Lucille, but knew if it wasn't for Valerie, she would no longer be here to enjoy these treasured moments together.

So Lily would show her appreciation, by momentarily leaving her beloved wall of soft moss, climb onto Valerie's lap, and rub the soft fur of her cheek against Valerie's hand, just to show her how truly valued she was.

Weather permitting, they would make their way to the highest peak of the cliff, watching nature's own watercolors paint the skies with amber golds, until the sun dipped into the rhythmic percussion of the waves. Corbiere lighthouse would always be a constant beacon of light to Lucille and Lily, and no matter what the storms may bring, there would always be the guiding light of the lighthouse that would bring them safely home. And any friendship, furry or otherwise, could and would, weather any storm, and find a path to true happiness and love.

Epilogue

The story of Raymond and Dorothy was, and always will be, a true love story, they possessed a love so deep and unwavering, that it endured beyond the limits of time, distance and mortality, because they still exist in the hearts and minds of all of our family.

I sometimes close my eyes, and I can once again see my Grandad pottering around in his garden, walking up the winding concrete path past his greenhouse, surrounded by verdant foliage and vibrant flowers, immersed in the serene tranquility of his own botanical oasis.

My Gran would be standing in the kitchen window preparing freshly picked vegetables from the garden, or making jam that would be bubbling away on the stove.

My favorite part of the week was a Sunday, for this was when we would visit our Grandparents, we would come charging in through the side of the bungalow door into the kitchen, which was always beautifully clean and well organized.

We would be greeted by my Gran, who always had that same reassuring smell, she didn't like anything scented or decadent, she had a papery clean smell like soap and hardbound books, which I always found pleasant and comforting.

I love how they pulled us into their familiar routine, tea and rich tea biscuits on arrival, then we would play in the garden, or if it was raining, we would sit and play with their treasures and ornaments. My favorite thing was a beautiful old church with stained glass windows, and when you turned the tiny ratchet on the back, it would play the most enchanting melody.

My Grandad would come back in from the garden, and would be seated in his favorite armchair in the corner of the lounge, Gran would appear, and soften the butter on the mantle of the electric fire, and then we would be beckoned to the dining room table. The food was always the same, Jam on bread, Madeira cake, and tinned peaches with carnation milk.

And that is how I remember them both, my Grandad with his utterly charismatic charm, and debonair demeanor, even out in the garden digging up his jersey royals he looked completely dashing.

My Gran however, was reserved and unassuming, and modest in her appearance, however, under those demure knee length skirts, and wooly cardigans, there was a hidden strength not visible to all.

104

And although my Grandad would never admit it, she was the rock that held them firm, and kept their marriage sailing on calm seas.

Sadly so, after over fifty years of marriage, my Grandad was the first to pass away. I still remember the day of the funeral, my Gran standing strong and steady at the front of the church. I don't think she was aware of anything around her, it was as if everything had stopped, as if in a photograph-two dimensional.

But once back in their bungalow, in an extended moment, she looked peaceful and calm as she looked out of the window, gazing at the flowers that Raymond her husband had planted for her. I think at that moment she realized he was not gone, just out of reach for now.

It was years later when Dorothy finally left this world to join her beloved Raymond, reunited once again, where they remained together for eternity.

My Mum visits their place of rest regularly, and not only does she take freshly cut flowers, but some bread too, for it seems that they gained the most unusual, yet apt guardian, in the form of a little Robin that keeps a watchful eye over them both.

I think he must have known that my Grandad was a gardener, a protector of the land, who brightened the lives of those around him with his beautiful and fragrant blooms.

It does seem that when we are in our younger years we travel through time at an alarming pace, but as you get older, you wonder what was it that shaped the person you became, and that is when I took one step back into the past, and realized that my future and the opportunities that I was bestowed, were down to two pretty amazing people, that not only gave me the most wonderful Mum, but a wonderful life too.

The End

Printed in Dunstable, United Kingdom